SHORT TALES
Furlock & Muttson Mysteries

THE CASE OF
THE HAUNTED HOUSE

by Robin Koontz

visit us at www.abdopublishing.com

Published by Magic Wagon, a division of the ABDO Group, 8000 West 78th Street, Edina, Minnesota, 55439. Copyright © 2010 by Abdo Consulting Group, Inc. International copyrights reserved in all countries. All rights reserved. No part of this book may be reproduced in any form without written permission from the publisher.

Short Tales ™ is a trademark and logo of Magic Wagon.

Printed in the United States of America, North Mankato, Minnesota.
092009
012010

Written and illustrated by Robin Koontz
Edited by Stephanie Hedlund and Rochelle Baltzer
Interior Layout by Kristen Fitzner Denton
Book Design and Packaging by Shannon Eric Denton

Library of Congress Cataloging-in-Publication Data

Koontz, Robin Michal.
    The case of the haunted house / written and illustrated by Robin Koontz.
        p. cm. -- (Short tales. Furlock & Muttson mysteries)
    ISBN 978-1-60270-560-9
    [1. Haunted houses--Fiction. 2. Halloween--Fiction. 3. Mystery and detective stories.] I. Title.
    PZ7.K83574Cash 2010
    [E]--dc22
                                                                    2008032540

"Good evening, Furlock!" said Muttson.
There was no answer.
"Furlock, where are you?"
"Boooooooooooo!" said a voice.

"Yikes!" Muttson cried.
"It is me, in my Halloween costume!" said
Furlock. "Did I scare you?"
"Yes, you did," said Muttson.

"Now you have to come with me. We have a case!"
"What is the case?" Furlock asked.
"Dame Bellington says that her house is haunted," said Muttson.

"We should go there right away!" Furlock said.
"Yes, we should," Muttson said. He shivered.
"What is the matter with you?" Furlock asked.
"Are you afraid of a haunted house?"

"No way," Muttson said.
He grabbed a bag from the closet.
"I will fire up the Furlock-Mobile!"

Furlock and Muttson drove through
the woods to the Bellington house.
They knocked on the door.
It slowly creaked open.

"Greetings!" said Dame Bellington.
"You must be Furlock and Muttson!"
"At your service," Furlock said.
"Please follow me," said Dame Bellington.

Dame Bellington led Furlock and Muttson to the kitchen.
"I see a Halloween pumpkin," Furlock said.
"Watch this," said Dame Bellington.

She opened a window.
"Mooooooan!" said the pumpkin.
"Yikes!" Muttson cried.
He pulled a device from the bag and held it
over the pumpkin.

"What is that?" Furlock asked.

"It is a Sound Level Meter," said Muttson.

"I am testing the pumpkin to see if it is haunted."

"The pumpkin is not haunted," Furlock said.

"That sound was wind blowing through the face holes."
"Oh," said Muttson.
"But that is not all," said Dame Bellington.
"There is more. Please follow me."

Dame Bellington led Furlock and Muttson to the living room.

"Watch the lamp on the table," said Dame Bellington.

She began to dance.

The lamp blinked in time to her steps.
"Yikes!" Muttson cried.
He pulled another device from the bag and held
it over the lamp.

"What is that?" Furlock asked.
"This is a Zap Checker," said Muttson.
"I am testing the lamp to see if it is haunted."

"The lamp is not haunted," said Furlock.
"It blinks because Dame Bellington is dancing on the cord."
"Oh," said Muttson. "Dame Bellington, you must never put a cord under a rug."

"But that is not all," said Dame Bellington.
"There is more. Please follow me."
Dame Bellington led Furlock and Muttson up
some stairs.

"There is a cold spot in this room," she said.
Muttson pulled another device from the bag.
He walked to the middle of the room.

"What is that?" Furlock asked.
"It is a Cold Spot Detector," said Muttson.
"I am testing this spot to see if this room is
haunted."

"The cold can be explained," said Furlock.
"Well then, what is that?" Dame Bellington
asked. She pointed to a dark corner behind
Furlock.
Light circles bounced up and down.

"Yikes!" Furlock cried.
"What do we have here?" asked Muttson.
He walked to the dark corner behind Furlock.
The light circles bounced to Furlock.
They bounced up and down around her head.

"Let's get out of here!" Furlock cried.
She ran down the stairs.
Dame Bellington followed.

"Come down, Muttson!" said Furlock.
There was no answer.
"Muttson, where are you?"
"Booooooooooo!" said a voice.
"Yikes!" Furlock cried.

"Did I scare you?" Muttson asked.
"Yes, you did," said Furlock. "How did you get under the stairs?"

"I used the trapdoor," Muttson said.
"What trapdoor?" asked Furlock.
"The one with the holes letting in cold air,"
said Muttson.

"Oh," said Furlock. "Then what were those bouncing lights?"

"Dust bunnies," said Muttson.

"Bunnies?" Furlock asked. She licked her lips.

"Not real bunnies," said Muttson. "Dust bunnies are clumps of dust that can fly."
"How come they lit up and bounced at me?" Furlock asked.
Muttson pointed to a light under the stairs.

"Oh, I see!" said Dame Bellington.
"The wind made the light swing and shine
through the holes in the trapdoor," said
Muttson.

"I do need to dust more often," Dame Bellington
said. She wiped her hands on her dress.
"I guess that means my house is not haunted!"
she said. "Here, have some Halloween candy."

"Booooooooooo!" said a voice.

"Yikes!" Muttson cried.

"Muththon, on thoo thuh neth caseth!" cried
Furlock.

"I am right behind you," said Muttson.

They jumped into the Furlock-Mobile
and sped away.